DOUBLE REVERSE

FRED BOWEN *series*
SPORTS STORY

FRED BOWEN SPORTS STORY series

DOUBLE REVERSE

FRED BOWEN

Ω
PEACHTREE
ATLANTA

Published by
PEACHTREE PUBLISHERS
1700 Chattahoochee Avenue
Atlanta, Georgia 30318-2112
www.peachtree-online.com

Cover design by Tom Gonzalez and Nicola Carmack
Composition by Melanie McMahon Ives

Printed in May 2014 by RR Donnelley and Sons in Harrisonburg, VA, U. S. A.
10 9 8 7 6 5 4 3 2 1
First Edition

Library of Congress Cataloging-in-Publication Data

Bowen, Fred.
  Double reverse / by Fred Bowen.
     pages cm
ISBN 978-1-56145-814-1 (hardcover)
ISBN 978-1-56145-807-3 (paperback)
  Summary: Although he knows all the plays, freshman wide receiver Jesse is reluctant to try out for quarterback until his brother, a college player, is asked to switch from quarterback to safety and the two make a deal that will force them, and Savannah, the new kicker on Jesse's team, to conquer their own and others' expectations.
  [1. Football—Fiction. 2. Ability—Fiction. 3. Brothers—Fiction. 4. Self-confidence—Fiction. 5. Sex role—Fiction.] I. Title.
  PZ7.B6724Dou 2014
  [Fic]—dc23
                                   2014006500

For Clare Elizabeth Bowen.

Welcome.

Chapter 1

Ready…set…hut one!" Jesse Wagner and his older brother Jay were running pass patterns at Hobbs Park, just as they had a thousand times before. Jesse was always the wide receiver and Jay was always the quarterback.

Jay crouched as if he was taking the ball from the center.

Jesse bolted from the line of scrimmage and dashed straight downfield. His sweat-stained T-shirt and baggy gym shorts flapped in the hot summer breeze.

Jesse counted in his head. At the count of three, he faked left, dug his cleat into the dry playground dirt, and broke sharply to the right. The football was already spinning toward him. He reached up and snagged the perfect spiral with two hands, then stutter-stepped to keep both feet inside the faded chalk sideline.

"First down!" Jay called out, thrusting his hand downfield like a referee. "Nice catch."

Jesse turned and jogged back. He snapped off a quick pass as he ran. "Good pass," he said, stopping on the line of scrimmage. "It was in the perfect spot—to the outside, away from the defender."

Jay crouched down again. "Let's run the same deep-out pattern a few more times. I need to practice that one."

Jesse set up at his wide-receiver position with his hands on his hips. He looked over at his brother.

Jay was standing on an empty field in the steamy August sun wearing shorts and a T-shirt. But gripping the football in front of him, he still looked every inch a quarter-back. Jay was taller than Jesse, almost six foot two, and much stronger. He was four years older, and in a few days, he'd be heading off for his freshman year at Dartmouth College.

"Ready...set...hut one!"

The two brothers practiced the deep-out pattern over and over. Sweat poured down Jesse's face and he could feel the salt stinging his eyes.

Finally Jay declared that he'd had enough. He and Jesse walked to the sideline, splashed water on their faces, and wiped them dry with ragged towels.

"You're looking good today," Jesse said. "I wish I could throw like that."

Jay shrugged. "My hands are kind of sweaty. I couldn't get a good grip on some of the deep-out passes."

"They looked all right to me."

The empty field simmered in the sun. Jay spun the football in his hands. "I've got to put more zip on the ball," he said, his voice taking on a serious tone. "The college game is a lot faster. And the defensive backs are much better than the guys I played against in high school."

"So practice starts Monday?" Jesse asked.

"Yeah. Mom and Dad are driving me up Sunday morning."

"But classes don't start for a week or two?"

"Right. We have a heavy practice schedule for a while. This college football thing is pretty serious."

"You'll show 'em," Jesse said. "You were the best quarterback Franklin High School ever had. No way those other college guys are as good as you. You were All-Conference twice. You set records for passing yards and touchdown passes—"

"Whoa, whoa, whoa, little bro!" Jay laughed. "Maybe you should write the coach. Tell him you've been running pass patterns for me for years and I'm the best quarterback you've ever seen."

"It's true. Where's my phone? I'll text him right now."

"That was just high school," Jay said, waving Jesse off. "Believe me, a lot of college players were big shots in high school. I'll be starting all over again." Jay tossed Jesse a short pass. "Come on, let's get out of here."

They headed toward the gate on the other side of the park. "When does football start for you?" Jay asked.

"In a couple of weeks."

"Who's coaching the freshman team this year?"

"Mr. Butler."

"Oh yeah, he was an assistant with the junior varsity when I started out." Jay slapped Jesse in the stomach with the back of his hand. "He's a good coach. He'll get you in shape."

"Hey! I *am* in shape," Jesse protested, tightening his stomach muscles. "From running all those pass patterns for you."

"You'll find out if you are soon enough," Jay said.

"I wonder if they'll change any of the plays in the playbook."

"Probably not. The varsity, JV, and freshman teams run pretty much the same stuff," Jay said and then dropped back three quick steps. "Quick fly!"

Jesse darted downfield, and Jay flipped him a pass that hit him in stride. Jesse tucked the ball under his arm and sprinted away.

"Touchdown!" Jay ran down the field after his brother. "At least you won't have to spend any time learning the plays," he said as Jesse tossed the ball back. "You already know them all."

Jesse fell into step with his brother. "I used to quiz you on them all the time," he said. "Remember?"

Jay nodded, then faked a handoff and faded back. Jesse flared out to the right and Jay tossed him a soft pass.

The brothers talked and tossed the football back and forth in the late summer heat, just as they'd done so many times before.

"So have you decided what position you're going to try out for?" Jay asked.

"Wide receiver."

"You'll make a good one."

Jesse thought about the Franklin High School freshman team. "I just hope I have a quarterback who's half as good as you."

Jesse dug his cleats into the practice field turf and broke sharply to the right. He looked back for the pass.

The football whistled above his outstretched hands. Too high.

Jesse hustled over to pick up the ball. As he jogged back, he threw a perfect spiral to Coach Vittone, Franklin High School's longtime assistant football coach. Even though Coach Vittone was bald, wore glasses, and was a lot older than Coach Butler, he still looked as solid as a linebacker.

"Get your throws down, Henry!" Coach Butler barked. His curly hair was tucked under a blue Franklin High School baseball cap, and his arms were crossed tight against his chest. "Come on, get back to the huddle. Let's run another one."

Jesse stood next to Quinn Doherty, his best friend and the Panthers' big right tackle. Coach Butler leaned into the huddle. "Let's run Wide Dig, Flare Right." The pass play instantly appeared in Jesse's mind just as it was drawn in the Franklin High School playbook.

Henry Robinson, the Panthers' starting quarterback, glanced at Coach Butler as if he wasn't sure what he had said.

"The right end runs a square-in pattern and the halfback flares right." Jesse could hear the impatience in Coach Butler's voice. "Come on, call it!"

Henry repeated the play call. Jesse thought about Henry as he trotted out to his right-end position. *He's like Jay: tall, athletic, and can throw the ball a mile. Henry looks like a quarterback. I just wish he played more like one.*

"Ready...set...hut one...hut two!"

Jesse bolted from the line of scrimmage. Ten yards downfield he faked right and cut left over the middle of the field. But Henry's throw was way off. Jesse didn't have a chance.

The Panthers' practice continued in the bright September sunshine until sweat darkened the players' light gray practice jerseys. Coach Butler was putting the boys through their paces: Sprints. Running plays. Pass patterns. Blocking drills. Tackling drills.

"Watch the tackling," Coach Vittone cautioned the players. "Remember, we don't want to get anybody hurt in practice."

Finally Coach Butler blew his whistle. "All right. Water break. Everybody drink up. It's getting hot out here."

They all headed to the sidelines, gulping from their water bottles. Jesse stood with Quinn and Langston Dunn, another friend and a Panther reserve wide receiver. Quinn was much taller than Jesse, but he *really* towered over Langston.

Langston was gazing across the practice field to the school tennis courts, where the Franklin girls' team was practicing in their crisp tennis whites. "Maybe I should play tennis instead of football," he sighed.

"What are you talking about?" Quinn asked, taking another gulp of cold water.

Langston opened his hands toward the tennis courts. "Look at 'em," he said. "They aren't even sweating out there."

"So what?"

"So look at us."

Jesse's jersey was soaked with grimy sweat. Quinn's was even worse.

Jesse grinned and looked him up and down. "You look like someone threw you into a swimming pool." He enjoyed teasing the big lineman.

"I wish someone would." Quinn took another long drink of water and wiped his mouth with his dirty sleeve.

"I must have run a million pass patterns today," Jesse sighed. "And I only caught two or three balls. Tops."

"Yeah," Langston agreed. "Henry throws it all over the place."

"But he sure acts like he's an All-Pro," Jesse said, thinking about how Henry ordered the players around the practice field.

"An All-Pro would know the plays," Langston said. "Coach has to tell Henry what the plays mean almost every time."

"Quit complaining," Quinn said. "At least you guys aren't stuck in the line, knocking into people the whole time. You have it easy, running around and catching balls."

Jesse splashed some water across his forehead and looked up at Quinn. "You know why coaches always put you in the line? Because you're so big and you can block other guys. Heck, you block out the sun. You just *look* like a lineman."

"I guess I look like a bench warmer," Langston said, "because that's where the coaches always put me."

"All right, guys!" Coach Butler shouted, clapping his hands. "Let's have two laps around the field. Then we'll see you tomorrow. Same time. Be ready to work hard."

Jesse, Quinn, and Langston jogged around the field behind their quarterback Henry and a few other Panther players. The clatter of shoulder pads bouncing on their shoulders was the only sound in the warm, windless air.

Halfway through the second lap, Jesse glanced over at Quinn and Langston. "Come on," he said. "Let's sprint it!"

Jesse and Langston burst away, with Quinn following closely behind them. They blew by Henry and the others, yelling and screaming as they ran.

"Come on, slowpokes!"

"Eat my dust, Panthers!"

"Last one in has to smell Quinn's gear!"

Jesse and Langston ran ahead of the others, neck and neck. With just ten yards to go, Jesse turned on the jets and his longer stride pulled him into the lead. He flashed into the end zone just one yard ahead of Langston.

"That wasn't fair," Henry protested when he crossed the line a few moments later. "You guys snuck up on us."

Langston laughed. "You could have started sprinting sooner," he said. "There's no rule against it. You're just being sore losers."

The team clomped into the locker room, their cleats clacking on the hard floor. Jesse stopped in front of the Franklin High School football schedules—varsity, junior varsity, and freshman—on the Big Board above the locker room door. He studied the freshman schedule.

FRANKLIN HIGH SCHOOL FRESHMAN TEAM
[all games on Thursdays]

Date	Team	Time	Score
9/19	South Shore	3:30 p.m.	
9/26	@ Pinewood	3:30 p.m.	
10/3	Glen Forest	3:30 p.m.	
10/10	Roosevelt	3:30 p.m.	
10/17	@ Auburn	3:30 p.m.	
10/24	@ Morgan	3:30 p.m.	
10/31	@ St. Andrews	3:00 p.m.	
11/7	Eastport	3:00 p.m.	

"Lotta games," Quinn said, staring at their schedule.

Yeah, Jesse thought. *Especially when we don't have a quarterback who can throw a decent pass.*

Chapter 3

Jesse sat with his head down, sipping his soda through a plastic straw. Langston checked his phone. "Hurry up, Jesse. You eat slower than my grandmother."

"Yeah, I thought you needed to go to Mike's Sporting Goods," Quinn said.

The three boys sat in the food court at the lower level of Eastport Mall. Above them, shoppers with bulging bags buzzed around the second and third levels.

"I didn't think it was going to be so crowded," Jesse said. Then he went back to sipping his soda. Very slowly. "Maybe we should come back tomorrow."

"Come on," Quinn said. "It's a mall. It's always crowded. You gotta buy one. You're the guy who lost it."

"Yeah, and you wouldn't want to play football without it." Langston slid out of the booth.

Jesse took one last noisy slurp of soda and stood up. "Okay, let's go."

The three boys headed over toward the escalator.

"Think we'll be ready for Thursday's game?" Langston asked.

Jesse shrugged. "I don't think we'll score much. Henry hasn't gotten any better at quarterback. He still doesn't know the plays and he throws the ball all over the place."

"Griffin will get us some yards," Langston said. "He's a good runner."

"Yeah, he's a good running back, but..." Jesse's voice trailed off. He wasn't so sure about the Panthers' chances.

"At least you've got a chance to touch the ball," Quinn grumbled. "When you're in the line, the only time you touch the ball is if somebody fumbles."

"So what?" Lanston said, "I'm stuck on the bench...a second-stringer behind this guy." He seized Jesse playfully by the shoulders.

"Maybe I should push him off this escalator!" Langston yelled out. "So I'd get a chance to play for a change."

Quinn laughed. "No way. You can't kill Jesse before the season starts. We may need him."

As they approached the sports shop, Jesse stopped and grabbed Quinn by the elbow. "Look at this place," he whined. "It's packed. Let's get out of here."

Quinn shook Jesse loose. "Stop being such a baby."

"Hey, look. There's Savannah Harris." Langston pointed to a tall girl who was looking over a display case filled with soccer goalie gloves.

Jesse could feel the blood rushing to his face. "Man, I definitely don't want to buy it with her around."

Langston headed straight for the goalie glove case. "Hi, Savannah," he said. "Soccer season started yet?"

"Hey, Langston." Savannah smiled down at him, then slipped her hands into some goalie gloves. "Starts next Saturday."

Quinn went over to join them. Jesse hung back behind Quinn, hoping Savannah wouldn't see him.

"Hey, guys," Savannah said. "What are you all here for?"

"Jesse's got to buy something for football," Quinn said, sliding to one side so she could see him.

Jesse could feel the heat in his face again. He wished he had stayed at home.

"Why are you looking at goalie gloves?" Langston asked. "I thought you played defense...in the field."

Savannah shook her head. "Coach Oliver stuck me in the goal."

"You like playing goalie?" Langston asked.

"Not really. I like scoring goals more than I like stopping goals. But Coach thought it might be a good spot for me. He's always said I looked like a goalie. You know, because I'm so tall."

Quinn laughed. "Sounds familiar," he said. "Our coaches do the same thing. You know, put you in a position because of how you look."

Savannah pulled on a white pair of gloves with neon yellow fingers and spun toward Jesse. "How do you like these?" she asked, holding up her hands.

Startled, Jesse stumbled over his words. "Great...great. I'm sure they'll look...great." He just wanted to get out of the store.

"Hey, Savannah, what color's your goalie shirt?" Langston asked.

"Bright yellow. I look like I'm leading the Tour de France."

"Then those will go *great*." Langston smiled. "Just like Jesse said."

"Since when did you two get to be such big fashion experts?" Quinn asked.

Savannah smiled. "I'm all set, then. You guys were a big help. Do you want me to help you to pick out something, Jesse? What are you buying?"

"I...I don't think so," he stammered. "I'm cool...no worries."

Langston and Quinn covered their mouths to keep from laughing.

"What's so funny?" Savannah asked.

Quinn was almost gasping for breath.

"Jesse's got to buy a protective cup for football."

Jesse froze. It was as if his mouth had quit working.

"Well, I'm sure you don't want to play football without that," Savannah said.

"You've got that right," Langston said. He and Quinn giggled like a couple of second-graders.

"Come on, let's buy this thing and get out of here," Jesse said finally, pulling his two teammates away.

"When's your first game?" Savannah called out.

"Thursday at 3:30. It's a home game," Jesse answered. He was relieved to be talking about anything but what he was there to buy.

"Who are you playing?"

"South Shore. You should drop by," Langston said.

"Maybe I will."

The team crowded around Coach Butler after the second-half kickoff. "Come on, guys, we're down 14–0!" he shouted. "We've got to put some points on the board, quick."

Huddled with his teammates, Jesse thought back on the first half. The Panthers offense had struggled. Jesse had caught only one short pass. Most of Henry's pass attempts were either too high or too low. And without a passing attack, Griffin Puvel, the Panthers' top running back, had found it hard to gain many yards on the ground.

The Panthers' kicking game was even worse. Two short punts had given the South

Shore Sailors good field position, and they had roared down the field for easy scores.

Now, Coach Butler held a clipboard above his head.

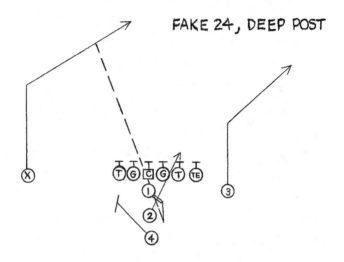

FAKE 24, DEEP POST

He smacked the tip of the marker against the diagrammed play as he explained it. "We're starting with Fake 24, Deep Post. Henry fakes to Griffin to hold the linebackers. Then Jesse runs a deep post over the middle. We may catch the defense napping. Run it right."

The Panthers offense jogged onto the field. Henry knelt down in the huddle and repeated Coach Butler's orders. "Fake 24, Deep Post on two!" he barked. "Run it right."

Jesse flanked out to the left. He rested his hands on his hip pads and dug his right foot into the turf. He was ready to take off.

"Ready...set...hut one...hut two!"

Jesse flew off the line, counting in his head. At three, he pushed off his left foot and angled to the goalposts at the far end of the field. Jesse's speed caught the Sailors defensive backs by surprise. He broke into the clear with nothing in front of him but green grass. As Jesse looked back for the pass, he was thinking *touchdown!*

But Henry's throw was too long, even for Jesse at top speed. The ball flew over his head and landed ten yards downfield. Jesse slowed to a disappointed jog. His chance for a touchdown was gone.

A run into the line gained only one yard. It was third down, nine yards to go for a first down. The Panthers needed someone to make a play.

"Middle Cross," Henry said.

The pass is coming to me, Jesse thought. The diagram of the play appeared in his mind. After the snap he sprinted 12 yards straight downfield and cut sharply into the middle of the field.

Just get the ball to me, Henry, and I'll take care of the rest.

Jesse broke into the clear for the briefest moment, but the pass was too late...and too high. He reached up and back, hoping he could somehow snag the ball out of the air. The football skimmed off the tips of his out-stretched fingers.

Wham! A Sailors defensive back cracked into Jesse's chest with his shoulder pads.

Whomp! Jesse's body snapped back and he fell hard.

Jesse lay in the dirt, out of breath from the solid hit. He slowly lifted himself to his elbows as the Sailors defense celebrated around him.

"Good defense!"

"Big hit!"

"Let's go, Sailors!"

Jesse struggled to his feet and headed toward the sideline. Coach Vittone met him before he was off the field. "Look at me," he ordered, resting his hands on Jesse's shoulders and staring straight into his eyes.

"What quarter is it?" he asked Jesse.

"Third."

"What's the score?"

"We're behind 14–0. I'm okay, Coach."

"Who's the other team?"

"The South Shore Sailors. Really, I'm fine."

Coach Vittone patted him on the shoulder. "Just wanted to be sure," he said. "You took a pretty hard lick." He turned and shouted to Coach Butler. "Jesse's okay! But let's sit him for at least the next set of downs."

Coach Butler nodded and turned his attention back to the game. Another short punt had put South Shore in good field position.

Jesse took off his helmet and sat on the Panthers' bench.

Quinn plopped down beside him. "You okay?" he asked.

"Yeah."

"Henry's gonna get you killed if he keeps throwing the ball high like that over the middle."

Jesse leaned forward and rested his elbows on his knees and his head in his hands.

Quinn smiled. "Good thing you bought that cup, or you'd really be in trouble."

Jesse hurt too much to laugh.

The Sailors drove downfield for another touchdown. Jesse checked the scoreboard.

The worst part of it was the zero below Panthers. The offense hadn't done a thing.

Jesse got up and walked gingerly back and forth along the sidelines, testing his aching muscles. He kept his eyes on the field. The Panthers had the ball and were trying desperately to score. Henry faded back to pass. Just as he released the ball, a Panther lineman stumbled and fell back into the quarterback, hitting him square between his knee and ankle.

"Aaaargh!" Henry crumpled to the ground and grabbed his right ankle.

The sidelines fell quiet as the coaches and the trainer ran out onto the field. The Panthers huddled near the edge of the field. After a couple of minutes, Coach Vittone and Quinn helped Henry limp to the sidelines.

"Kurt Fuller, get in there!" Coach Butler shouted. The Panthers' backup quarterback pulled on his helmet and trotted onto the field.

"Fuller's going in," Langston said in a low voice to Jesse as he snapped his chin strap tight. "Man, we're in the deep stuff now. He can't play a lick." Langston raced back to the huddle.

"Yeah," Jesse said to himself. "At least Henry *looked* like a quarterback."

Sure enough, the Panthers offense went

nowhere with Kurt at quarterback. Four plays later, Quinn and Langston were standing on the sidelines with Jesse.

"Man, 20–0," Quinn breathed, shaking his head. "I don't think Savannah will be real impressed with us."

"Was she here?" Langston asked. "Did you see her?"

"Yeah," Quinn said. "But I think she left at halftime."

"I don't blame her." Jesse watched the South Shore Sailors move steadily down-field for another score. "I wish I could leave too."

"You know what I wish?" Langston asked.

"What?"

Langston glanced at Jesse. "I wish Jay was your *twin* brother."

"Yeah," Jesse said, staring hopelessly at the field. "Then we'd have a *real* quarter-back."

Chapter 5

The late Sunday morning sunshine slanted through the window as Jesse's mother stepped quietly into his bedroom. She leaned over and gently shook his shoulder.

"We have a surprise for you," she whispered in his ear.

"Wha...what?" Jesse pulled his covers closer to his chin. He was still sleepy.

"Jay's home. He's in the kitchen."

Jesse opened his eyes and tossed the covers back. "All *right*!" He forgot about sleeping in and ran downstairs barefoot.

Jay was leaning against the kitchen counter in new dark green sweats. "Hey, champ!" he said. "How's my favorite wide receiver?"

Jesse gave his brother a quick hug. "What are you doing home? I thought you guys were practicing all the time."

"We were just talking about that," their father said. He didn't sound happy.

Jesse looked at Jay. Something was up. His brother was staring at the floor like he'd never seen the kitchen tiles before.

"It looks as though Jay's taking a little time off," Jesse's mother said softly.

"When does the coach want your decision?" their dad asked Jay, his voice still tense.

"He said I could think about it over the weekend," Jay said. "But I have to be at practice on Tuesday or I'm off the team."

Jesse's father pushed away from the kitchen table and began pacing the room. "Well, I don't think you should quit," he said, the words tumbling out. "You don't have to play quarterback. I think you would make a good safety. Seems like the coaches think so too."

Their mother put her hand on Jay's shoulder.

"What's going on?" Jesse looked from her

to his father and then back to his brother, searching for answers. "You aren't playing quarterback anymore? Are you quitting or something? I mean...what's going on?"

"The coaches want to make me into a defensive back," Jay said. "They want me to play safety."

"Are you kidding?" Jesse shouted. "You're a great quarterback. The best one Franklin High ever had!"

"They've got guys who are better." Jay shrugged. "A whole bunch of guys."

"Better than you?" Jesse couldn't believe that. No way anyone was better than his brother.

Jesse's question hung in the air for a moment.

Jay paused as if he didn't want to admit it, even to himself. "Yeah," he said finally. "Better than me."

"Teams need lots of players." Their father had calmed down a little. "Maybe you can help the team by knocking down passes instead of throwing them."

"You don't have to decide right now."

Jesse's mother smiled and elbowed her husband. "Why don't you get these guys something to eat?"

Their dad made his special scrambled eggs with home fries, and they all sat down for a late breakfast. For a while, everything seemed back to normal, like it had been when Jay was still home and still the quarterback.

Jesse's mom and dad quizzed Jay about his classes, friends, teammates, and roommates. They even wanted to know about the food at school.

Jay laughed after swallowing a big gulp of orange juice. "I can tell you one thing. I haven't had a breakfast like this for a long time."

"You should always start the day with a good breakfast," their mom said. Jesse and Jay traded a look that said they had heard that one before...a thousand times.

Everyone seemed happy for the moment, but the question of whether Jay would go back and play football hung over the kitchen table like a rain cloud.

The talk finally swung back around to

football. But to Jesse's team, not Jay's.

"How'd you guys do against South Shore?" Jay asked.

"We lost, 26–0."

"Ouch. How'd you do?"

"Not so great. I only caught one pass for about five yards. It was the only pass Henry got close to me." Jesse quickly added, "And I was wide open a bunch of times."

"Give Henry some time. Maybe he'll settle down."

"Doesn't matter if he does. He sprained his ankle real bad in the second half. He'll be out for at least a month."

"Ouch again. Who's his backup?"

"Kurt Fuller. He's worse than Henry."

"Triple ouch."

The boys cleared the table and put the breakfast dishes in the dishwasher.

"You want to go out and throw the ball around?" Jay asked.

"Sure."

In five seconds, they were out the door. Jesse had the football tucked under his arm. His quarterback was home.

Chapter 6

The morning was sunny and warm with just a breath of a cooling breeze. Perfect football weather.

"Want to go to Hobbs Park?" Jesse asked, already heading in that direction.

Jay sniffed the air. "Nah," he said, shaking his head. "Let's go to the beach. I think it's low tide."

The brothers broke into a silent jog. In a few minutes they were stepping onto the cool, hard sand of Preston Beach.

"See? I told you it'd be low tide," Jay said with a wide smile.

Jesse sat down and pulled off his sneakers and socks. "It doesn't feel right to wear sneaks on the beach."

Jay slipped off his shoes too. He gazed at the wide sweep of sand, the blue sky, and the bluer water. "I miss this place," he said. "There's nothing like it at school. Just a lot of woods. All those trees feel like they're closing in on you. The beach feels open." He held his arms out. "Wide open."

Without another word, the brothers lined up in their familiar positions: Jay at quarterback, Jesse at wide receiver.

Jay called out plays and pass patterns. Jesse ran square-ins, curl-ins, down-and-outs, and deep posts. Jay put pass after pass right in Jesse's hands. The football never touched the sand.

"All right," Jay said. "Let's run a deep-out."

Jesse took off down the beach. He faked left, dug his bare toes into the sand, and broke to the right. The football spun through the clear salt air right into Jesse's hands. He tossed it back to his brother.

"Break time." Jay stared out at the ocean. The sparkling water spilled onto the sand in small, rhythmic waves. "Let's go check out the water."

"You're throwing great," Jesse enthused as they headed down to the water's edge. "That last pass was right on the money."

"Not good enough, I guess," Jay said.

"Think you'll go back and play?" Jesse asked.

"I don't know. I've always been the quarterback." Jay let his feet sink into the soft, wet sand. A wave washed across his ankles. "Whoa! This water's freezing."

"You could be a good safety," Jesse said, ignoring the cold water splashing his shins. "You're a good athlete. You're fast enough. And you'll know what the quarterback is thinking. You'll probably intercept a million passes."

Jay peered out at the water as if the answer to his problem lay somewhere beyond the waves. He stepped a little further into the water. The ripples pooled around his ankles.

"What about you guys?" Jay asked. "Losing 26–0, that stinks. What's going on with your team?"

Jesse didn't feel like talking about the

Panthers. "We're not that bad," he said at last. "But it's tough when you don't have a decent quarterback."

Jay reached into the water and pulled up a smooth, flat stone. He leaned over and tossed it along the top of the waves. The stone skipped several times before ducking into the ocean.

"What about you?" Jay asked.

"What do you mean?"

"Why don't *you* play quarterback?"

"I'm not a quarterback," Jesse blurted out. "I'm not as big as you...and not half as strong."

Jay skimmed another stone across the water. "I don't know," he said. "You're really fast. You've got a good arm—"

"Not half as good as yours," Jesse insisted.

"You know the plays by heart," Jay said. "I think you could be a pretty good quarterback."

"No way. I'm a wide receiver, period."

Jay just stood there, watching the ocean roll in.

Jesse could sense that something had changed between the two of them. He wasn't sure exactly what or how. But now that Jay was talking about him being a quarterback, Jesse didn't feel quite so much like the little brother.

His brother skipped another stone along the top of the still surface. This time it bounced off the water eight or nine times before sinking.

"Tell you what," Jay said finally, turning to Jesse. "I'll make a deal with you. If you try out for quarterback, I'll go back and try playing safety."

Jesse thought about Jay's proposal. The Panthers needed a quarterback. And Kurt Fuller sure wasn't the answer.

Maybe Jay was right; maybe Jesse could play the position. After all, his brother should know. He was a quarterback. The best.

The sun was high. The ocean sparkled a deep green-blue. It felt like the last days of summer were holding on before the chill of autumn arrived.

"So what do you say?" Jay asked again. "Deal?"

Jesse turned to Jay and nodded. "Deal."

Jesse, Quinn, and Langston marched shoulder to shoulder through the halls of Franklin High School.

"You gonna ask him?" Quinn asked.

"I don't know," Jesse said. "I mean...I'm not really QB material."

Langston dismissed Jesse's second thoughts. "Don't put yourself down. You sure looked like a quarterback practicing with us yesterday afternoon."

"Even your brother said you were looking pretty good," Quinn added.

"That's just messing around and running patterns in the park." Jesse eyed his friends. "I mean, it's not like Quinn here is a real wide receiver."

"Hey, what do you mean?" Quinn frowned. "I caught almost every pass you threw me. I think I'd make a good tight end. If the coaches would let me." He gave Langston a good-humored shove. "And Langston was good too...for a little guy."

"I don't know...," Jesse repeated.

"Come on, you can't back down now," Quinn said, pushing open the door of the locker room. "You promised your brother, remember?"

Jesse remembered. He'd promised his brother again early that morning as Jay piled into the family car for the ride back to college.

Jay was keeping his part of the deal. Now it was time for Jesse to keep his.

"You gotta give it a try, man," Langston said. He lowered his voice so none of the other freshman players could hear him. "You're *way* better than Kurt."

When Jesse stepped out onto the practice field, he saw Coach Butler and Coach Vittone talking together.

"Now's your chance," Quinn insisted.

Jesse could feel Quinn's hand on his back. "Okay, okay. Quit pushing." Jesse took a deep breath. It was now or never.

"Hey, Coach!" Jesse hoped his greeting didn't sound too cheery.

Coach Butler looked up from his clipboard. "Hey, Jesse! Ready to work hard today?"

"Yeah, but—" Jesse took a deep breath. "I was kind of wondering, you know, if I could try playing quarterback. You know, now that Henry is hurt and everything?"

Coach Butler looked surprised. "You ever played quarterback?" he asked.

"Not exactly, but I practiced all this weekend with Quinn as my tight end and Langston as wide receiver. My brother Jay said I've got a good arm. Not great, but pretty good. And I know the playbook. I used to quiz Jay on it all the time."

"Your brother was a real good quarterback," Coach Vittone said. "One of the best high school quarterbacks I've ever—"

"Yeah," Coach Butler interrupted. "But he was a lot bigger...taller. I mean..." He paused as if he didn't want to hurt Jesse's feelings.

"I don't know," Coach Vittone mused. "Some quarterbacks aren't that big. Drew Brees isn't very tall. And that kid Wilson out in Seattle is pretty short." The older coach reached back into his grab bag of football memories.

"Think about Fran Tarkenton. He was an average-sized guy. Ended up in the Hall of Fame. Threw for more than 340 TDs...took a couple teams all the way to the Super Bowl." He chuckled. "They called him 'the Mad Scrambler' because of the way he moved around in the backfield."

The smile disappeared from Coach Vittone's face and he got serious. "Jesse here's got some speed. And what does it matter whether he *looks* like a quarterback so long as he *plays* like a quarterback?"

Coach Butler rubbed his chin, thinking over the idea.

"Might be worth a try," Coach Vittone said.

"You say you know the playbook?" Coach Butler asked.

"Yes sir. Backwards and forwards."

Butler rubbed his chin again, a little harder. "Okay," he said finally. "We'll let you run some plays today. See how you do. Now get warmed up."

Quinn and Langston were on Jesse the moment he joined the warm-ups. "Are they gonna let you try?" Quinn asked.

"Yup."

"All right!"

After the usual warm-ups and drills, Coach Butler gathered the players in a circle. "Let's run some plays. Kurt, you're at quarterback. Defense, remember: no tackling. Just engage the ball carrier. Okay, let's go."

Kurt ran about a dozen plays. Most of his passes fell incomplete. The offense looked ragged. It was as if they were all on different pages of the playbook. Jesse lined up at wide receiver again, wondering when he would get his chance at quarterback.

After another one of Kurt's overthrown passes, Coach Butler called out, "Langston! Take Jesse's place at wide receiver. Jesse, you go in for Kurt. Come on, hustle up. Look sharp!"

Jesse saw that Kurt was surprised. So was the rest of the team. The players in the huddle looked from side to side, not sure what was going to happen next. The coach leaned into the huddle and said, "Why don't we start with I-34."

Jesse felt a little funny doing the talking instead of the listening. He repeated the play in a strong voice, trying to sound as much like Jay as he could.

"Ready...set...hut one!" Jesse spun and handed the ball to Griffin, the Panthers' running back.

"Good job," Coach Butler said as the offense huddled up. "Run the pitch-right play."

Jesse realized that Coach was purposely not naming the play to test him. But it didn't matter anyway. Jesse knew exactly what to call from all the times he had quizzed Jay about the Franklin High School playbook.

"38 Power Sweep!" Jesse called. He could

see both Coach Butler and Vittone nodding with approval as the offense lined up.

Jesse called more running plays. With every down he felt more comfortable handling the ball and the offense.

"Quinn, move over to tight end. Mason, come in and play tackle!" Coach Butler looked at Jesse and lowered his voice. "Let's try a pass. Call what you feel comfortable with."

Jesse studied the faces of the players in the huddle. They were waiting for him to show the way. "Flood Pass Right on one."

The players got into their stances. Jesse looked over the defense and crouched behind the center.

"Ready...set...hut one!" Jesse dropped back and looked right for Langston running a down-and-out. A defensive end crashed through the line and into the backfield. Jesse spun away from the tackler and kept his eyes downfield. Langston was covered but Jesse spied Quinn open on a curl-in. Jesse flipped him a quick pass for an eight-yard gain.

44

Tweeeeeeeet!

Coach Butler blew his whistle. "Good play," he said, clapping his hands. "That's how we keep moving, Jesse! Good catch, Quinn. We're clicking now. Let's keep it going."

A couple of completions later, Coach Butler put Kurt back in to try again. Jesse sprinted to the sidelines, satisfied that he'd taken his first small steps to becoming a quarterback.

Coach Vittone clapped him on the shoulder pads. "Good job. The way you were scrambling around out there, you looked like a regular Fran Tarkenton."

"Yeah, I felt pretty good," Jesse said.

"We've got a lot of work to do to get you ready for Thursday."

"You mean...?"

"I'll talk to Coach Butler about having you start."

Jesse could feel a smile spreading across his face.

"Don't be too happy, Tark," Coach Vittone warned. "It won't be easy. Pinewood is tough."

Jesse didn't care. He was just glad for the chance. He looked at Coach Vittone and smiled. "Then I guess we'll find out on Thursday if I can play the part."

esse sat on the bench, staring at the play Coach Vittone had diagrammed on the clipboard. The cheers of the crowd and the Franklin High School freshman cheerleaders filtered through the ear holes in his helmet.

FAKE 34, ROLLOUT RIGHT

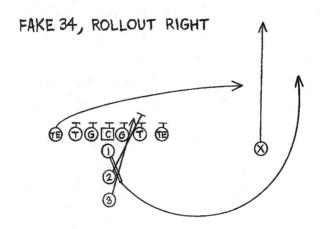

"It's like Fake 34, Pass, except instead of dropping back, you roll out to the right," the coach explained. "If you don't have an open receiver, you can run with it. We've got to take advantage of your speed."

Jesse nodded. He could still feel the butterflies in his stomach.

Coach Vittone patted him on the knee. "You're doing fine, Tark. We've still got a chance to win this one. Be ready after the defense stops them."

Coach Vittone was right. The Panthers were still in the game. Jesse took a few deep breaths as the Franklin defense tried to halt the Pinewood drive. He thought back over the first three quarters.

Franklin had received the opening kickoff, but the Panthers couldn't move the ball. The butterflies in Jesse's stomach had really been bad during the first few plays. A short punt had put Pinewood at midfield. They'd driven downfield, grinding out yards on the ground, for the first score.

"Look," Jesse had said to Quinn as the Pinewood placekicker trotted out onto the field. "They've even got a kicker."

"I wish *we* had one," Quinn had replied as the ball split the uprights.

The Panthers fell behind, 7–0.

The second time Franklin had the ball, Jesse dropped back to pass, but seeing nobody open, he took off. Scrambling by tacklers, Jesse picked up 12 yards.

First down!

After a couple of runs by Griffin and another first down, the Panthers had stalled. Another short punt led to a second Pinewood touchdown. The score was 14–0 at the half.

But when the Panthers got the ball near the beginning of the second half, they started moving. Mixing short passes and runs, Franklin marched straight downfield to the Pinewood ten-yard line. Jesse faked a handoff to Griffin and stepped back. The moment he saw Langston open in the corner of the end zone, he fired.

Touchdown!

Jesse had jumped so high in the air, he could've dunked a basketball.

Now, late in the second half with the game winding down, the scoreboard told the story.

WILDCATS 14 7:00 QTR 4 PANTHERS 6

The Panthers trailed 14–6 with seven minutes to go. Jesse sat on the bench waiting for another chance. He was feeling more comfortable in his new position. After the touchdown pass to Langston, the butterflies in Jesse's stomach had settled down. Led by Jesse's passing and Griffin's running, the Franklin offense had been moving the ball but couldn't put another score on the board.

The Franklin sidelines burst into cheers. The defense had held. It was fourth down. The Wildcats had to punt. Jesse jumped to his feet and clapped his hands.

Shouts came from all around him.

"They've got to kick it!"

"Let's go offense, get ready!"

"Comeback time!"

Jesse squirted water into his mouth and pulled on his helmet. The offense was going back on the field. Coach Vittone gave him an encouraging sign by shaking his fist. Jesse hurried into the huddle. "Fake 34, Rollout Right," he ordered.

Just as Coach Vittone had drawn it up, after the snap Jesse faked the ball to Griffin, went right and had a clear view of Langston. Jesse's pass hit him right on the numbers before he stepped out of bounds.

The referee signaled first down.

"Let's try it again," Jesse said back in the huddle. "You were wide open!"

This time the Pinewood defense had Langston covered. Jesse faked a pass and took off. He spun by a pair of Pinewood tacklers before he was brought down in Pinewood territory.

Jesse bounced up, clapping his hands. "All right, we're moving."

A few plays later, the Panthers were on

the 20-yard line. Jesse checked the clock: three and half minutes to go.

Jesse dropped back to pass but the pocket collapsed around him. He swerved to his right to avoid a blitzing linebacker. Jenesis Kerr, the Panthers' other wide receiver, had slipped behind the defense. Jesse reared back and let the ball fly. It settled into Jenesis's arms in the back of the end zone.

Touchdown! The Panthers were behind 14–12. They could tie it up with a 2-point conversion.

A Panther lineman ran in to the huddle breathlessly. "Coach says run Fake 33, Bootleg Right."

The coaches were putting the ball in Jesse's hands again.

The teams lined up at the three-yard line. "Ready...set...hut one!" Jesse faked a hand-off to Griffin and scooted to the right. Looking up, he saw that Langston was blanketed by the Pinewood defense. He spotted a sliver of an opening in the Pinewood line and decided to go for it. He darted to the left, bouncing off one tackler and spinning toward the end zone. He landed on his back. He wasn't sure he'd made it.

But his teammates let him know. They surrounded him and pulled him up, slapping his helmet and pads. He'd done it! The score was tied, 14–14!

A low, short kickoff allowed the Wildcats to get a good runback. Starting in Franklin territory, they drove downfield until they were on the doorstep of the Panthers end zone.

Jesse and the rest of the Franklin offense stood, cheering and hoping against hope that their defense would hold on.

"Dig in, defense!"

"Get tough! Need a stop."

"Hold that line! Hold that line!"

The cheers didn't help. The Wildcats fullback blasted over the goal line for another touchdown. The extra-point kick made it 21–14.

Jesse paced along the sidelines, getting himself and his offense fired up. "Come on, Panthers, let's go! We can do it! We've still got a minute left."

But Jesse never got back on the field. The Franklin kick returner fumbled the kickoff and Pinewood recovered. The Panthers lost, 21–14.

Jesse, Quinn, and Langston trudged off the field, the loss sticking to them like the dirt on their uniforms.

Jesse slapped his helmet against his thigh. "We should have beaten those guys. We had a chance."

Langston patted Jesse on the shoulder. "You're the one who gave us a chance. Good game, Tark."

"We're never going to win if we don't get our kicking game straightened out." Jesse sighed. "Every kickoff and punt was way short. It's like we're just giving yards away."

Quinn looked down at Langston. "How about you?" he asked. "Kickers are usually little guys, aren't they?"

"Don't look at me," Langston protested. "Just because I look like a kicker doesn't mean I am one."

"I wish you were," Jesse said. "We need a kicker big time."

eady...set...hut one!" Jesse faded back three steps, looked to his left, and fired a quick slant pass. Langston reached out and grabbed the ball in full stride.

"First down!" Langston spun the football in the playground grass. "Nice throw, Jess. Right on the money."

"How come you're always throwing to him?" Quinn complained as he jogged back to the line of scrimmage to get ready for another play.

Jesse held out his arms wide as if to take in the entire football field at Hobbs Park. "He's always open," he said.

"What? And I'm not?"

The three boys were practicing pass patterns and there were no defensive backs anywhere in sight.

"All right, all right," Jesse said, laughing. "I'll throw you one. Let's run Play Action, Waggle Out." He turned toward the backfield and explained the play. "Langston will line up at running back. I'll fake it to him and roll out, then hit you on a down-and-out."

"Do you want me to hold my block?" Quinn asked.

"Yeah, one count."

Jesse held the ball in front of him just the way Jay always did. Langston and Quinn lined up in three-point stance: Langston at running back, Quinn at tight end.

"Ready...set...hut one!"

The boys sprang into action. Jesse tucked the ball close to his body and spun left. He slipped the ball in and out of Langston's midsection and rolled out to the right.

Quinn pretended to block an imaginary defensive end, then took three quick, choppy steps downfield and broke to the right. While still on the run, Jesse flicked him a perfect spiral.

"Touchdown!" the big guy shouted as he sprinted under the goalposts. He spiked the ball into the grass.

"We finally won one!" Jesse raised his arms in victory.

Langston did his own celebration dance around the empty football field. "We finally found a team we could beat," he joked.

"Let's take a break," Quinn suggested. "I'm exhausted from playing against these nobodies."

Jesse peered toward the soccer pitch in the far corner of the park. "Why don't we check out the soccer game, see who's playing?" He waved his hand in a circle. "Come on, let's race."

The three teammates sped toward the soccer pitch. They arrived huffing and puffing. Jesse was first, then Langston, then Quinn.

"It's the freshman girls' team," Jesse said, surveying the field. "I think they're playing Eastport."

"Look," Langston said. "Savannah's in the goal."

With the action at the other end of the field, Savannah stood in her Day-Glo yellow goalie jersey about fifteen yards in front of her goal.

Langston cupped his hands and shouted, "Hey, Savannah! Nice gloves!"

She recognized the boys and waved.

Eastport got the ball and went on the attack. Savannah turned her attention back to the field. She snagged a crossing pass out of the air and waved her players away from the goal. After two short steps, she boomed a punt high and far downfield.

"Whoa!" Jesse said. "Did you see that kick?"

"Yeah," Quinn said. "It went past midfield."

Her next three punts were just as spectacular as the first. Watching Savannah got Jesse thinking.

An Eastport shot sailed over the net. Savannah retrieved the ball and placed it near the corner of the penalty area. She took a few confident steps forward and...

boom! The ball soared up the center of the field.

"Man, that girl can really kick!" Jesse exclaimed.

"A lot better than Denny," Langston said, referring to the freshman team's not-very-good kicker.

"That's what I was thinking," Jesse said softly to himself. He thought back to the season's many short punts and kickoffs that had put the Panthers in poor field position. He stared at Langston for a moment, then looked over at Quinn.

"Why don't we ask Savannah to be our kicker?" Jesse said, putting into words what he'd been thinking ever since he saw her blast that first kick.

"For starters, she's a girl," Quinn said.

"So what? Girls can play football."

"I don't know," Langston said. "She doesn't, you know, really look like a kicker."

"Yeah, and I don't look like a quarterback," Jesse said. Another of Savannah's punts sailed high into the air. "If you ask me, I'd say she looks a lot like a kicker."

"She can't play football," Quinn said. "She's already playing soccer."

"Why don't we ask her?" Jesse suggested. "Let her decide. She didn't sound crazy about playing the goal when we saw her at the mall."

"What about the other guys?" Quinn persisted. "Maybe they don't want a girl on the team."

"They want to win, don't they?" Jesse said. "If we're going to win, we need a kicker." Another one of Savannah's punts flew high in the air. "And she can really kick."

The last kick seemed to silence Quinn.

"All right, so who's gonna ask her?" Langston said.

"Mr. Quarterback," Quinn said, pointing at Jesse. "It's his big idea."

After the game, the three boys rushed up to Savannah and congratulated her on her team's win. After a minute, Jesse could feel Langston's hand on his back. "Go ahead, ask her," his friend whispered.

"Ask me what?" Savannah said.

"Well, you know, I was thinking...I mean, we were wondering," Jesse said, searching for the right words, "whether you would think about being the kicker—you know like the punter and stuff—for the freshman football team."

"Me?" She looked surprised. "On the football team?"

Quinn grabbed Jesse by the arm. "Let's go. I knew it was a stupid idea."

Savannah held up her gloved hands. "Hold on," she said. A small smile slid across her lips. "I think it could be kind of cool."

"Wait," Quinn said to the boys. "We don't even know if she can kick a football."

"Are you crazy?" Jesse shouted. "Were you watching that soccer game?"

"Quinn's right," Langston said. "Kicking a football is a lot different than kicking a soccer ball."

Savannah looked at the football under Jesse's arm. "There's only one way to find out," she declared. "I'll meet you at the football field at"—she checked her phone—"four o'clock."

When the three friends arrived at the football field, Savannah was waiting for them, still in her soccer uniform. "Hey," she said. "How do you want to do this?"

"Let's start with punting," Jesse suggested.

Quinn hiked the ball to Savannah and the soccer goalie boomed punts downfield to Jesse and Langston. With every punt, the boys grew more excited.

"Dude, she is *way* better than Denny."

"Whoa, fair catch, fair catch."

"Look at that! The girl has got serious hang time on her kicks."

After a while, Jesse pointed to the goalposts. "Do you think you can kick field goals?" he asked.

"No problem," Savannah said.

They set up for a 25-yard field goal.

Langston ran behind the end zone. "I'll stand back here so I can tell you whether the kick is good or not."

Quinn crouched down and stared back through his legs, ready to hike the ball. Jesse knelt on his left knee and held out his hands. Savannah stepped off the distance from the ball like an old pro. She looked at Jesse and nodded.

"Ready...set...hut one!"

Quinn hiked the ball.

Jesse spotted it.

Savannah stepped forward and...

Plunk!

The ball sailed end over end, arcing straight and true through the uprights. Langston threw his arms up to signal the kick was good.

Jesse looked at his teammates' surprised faces and smiled. "I think we've found ourselves a kicker."

Chapter 10

So we thought Savannah could be our kicker," Jesse said to Coach Butler and Coach Vittone.

Quinn and Langston stood in back of Jesse in full football gear. They had arrived early, a few minutes before their Monday practice. Savannah waited in gray sweats with her long brown hair pulled back.

"Are you serious?" Coach Butler sounded even less convinced than he had when Jesse asked to try out for quarterback.

"Yeah," Jesse insisted. "I mean, she can really boom it."

"She's got serious hang time, Coach," Langston added. "She's got a real strong leg. And hey, she's bigger than me." He looked around. "I know that's not saying much, but she is."

Coach Butler eyed Savannah. "What do *you* think?" he asked.

Savannah didn't even blink. "I think I can do it," she said.

"Have you ever played football?" Coach Vittone asked.

"Some. Touch football down at the park. And I did some punting and place kicking with these guys over the weekend."

"Ever play tackle football?"

"Yeah, with my older brothers...some-times."

"Was one of your brothers named Julius?" Coach Vittone asked. "I remember him, good player."

Savannah nodded, smiling. "Yeah, he could play."

"I don't know about this," Coach Butler said.

"Lots of girls play football," Jesse said. "I looked online last night and there are hundreds of them on high school teams. One girl even kicked the winning field goal for her school on the same night she was the Homecoming Queen."

"I don't want to be the Homecoming Queen," Savannah said. "I want to play football."

"Listen, I've got no problem with girls playing football." Coach Butler turned to Savannah. "But what about soccer? Aren't you the goalkeeper for the freshman team? What's Coach Oliver got to say about this?"

"I figured I'd try out before I talked to Coach Oliver." Savannah didn't sound quite so confident now. "Anyway, I thought it would be a lot more fun to score points instead of stopping goals."

Coach Butler looked at Coach Vittone. "What do you think?"

"It's worth a shot," Coach Vittone said in a low voice. "We definitely need an upgrade in our kicking game. But we'd need to clear it with Coach Oliver."

Coach Butler nodded toward the practice field where the rest of the team had begun to gather. "All right then. Guys, go get warmed up. And Savannah, can you stick around a few minutes? While the team's doing drills, Coach Vittone will see what you can do."

Jesse, Quinn, and Langston trotted onto the field. Jesse looked back and gave Savannah a thumbs-up sign.

"We'll need a couple of guys to set you up. How do you want to work this?" Coach Vittone asked Savannah.

"Well," she said. "Quinn's been my long snapper and Jesse's been my holder. So I would kind of like to use them. At least for the first few kicks."

Savannah began warming up by stretching along the sidelines. The team barely noticed her as they jogged with their heads down around the field. On the second lap, Griffin, the Panthers' running back, yelled out, "Hey, Savannah! You lost or something? This isn't the soccer pitch."

"She's not lost," Jesse said without slowing his pace. "She might be our kicker."

"No way. What are you talking about?" another Panther protested.

"Savannah. I think she's gonna be our

kicker. She can really boot it."

"A girl?"

"So what if she's a girl," Jesse said. "I'm telling you she's a kicker."

"Good," Griffin muttered. "We could use one."

During the warm-ups, Jesse saw that Coach Vittone had Savannah at the other end of the field, demonstrating the basics of punting a football.

Vittone waved from downfield. "Jesse? Quinn? Get over here!"

As they approached, Jesse heard the coach talking to Savannah. "Hold the laces away from your foot," he said. "Take two steps. Power your way through the ball."

Savannah went through the motions a couple of times.

"Okay then," Vittone said. "You guys get into position and let's give this a try."

Quinn was hiking from the 10-yard line, so Jesse set himself up at the 40-yard line. *A 30-yard kick would be pretty good*, he thought.

"Ready, Jesse?" called the coach. "Tell me

what yard line you're on when you catch the ball."

The first punt sailed in a tight spiral high above Jesse's head. He dashed back and caught the ball over his shoulder like a long pass. "The 47!" he yelled back. "That's a 37-yard kick."

Savannah's kicks kept on coming and Jesse kept on shouting out the yardages: 35 yards...39 yards...28 yards... Only one of the kicks fell too short for him to catch it.

Coach Vittone waved Jesse in.

"I told you she could kick," Jesse said breathlessly. He traded high fives with Savannah and Quinn.

"Let's try some field goals," Coach Vittone said. "We'll start with a few extra points."

Quinn hiked the ball from the three-yard line. Jesse spotted the ball at the ten-yard line. Savannah drove it through the uprights. No problem.

"It's good!" Jesse shouted.

After a few more kicks, they moved back five yards. Then another five yards. Now and then a kick was off line, but Savannah made enough of them to impress Coach Vittone. He smiled. He liked what he was seeing.

Coach Butler arrived just as a 35-yard field goal floated over the crossbar. "So what's the verdict?" he asked.

"We'd better find this girl a football uniform," Vittone said.

Jesse and Quinn let out a cheer. "All right! Way to go, Savannah! We've got ourselves a kicker."

Savannah undid her ponytail and shook out her hair around her shoulders. "I wonder if I should cut my hair," she said as if the thought had just occurred to her.

"Don't worry about that," Coach Butler assured her.

Jesse laughed. "Yeah. There are plenty of guys in the NFL with longer hair than you."

Chapter 11

The Franklin freshman team captains, Griffin and Quinn, ran back to the team huddle. "We're kicking off!" they shouted.

Jesse caught Savannah's eye. She didn't look nearly as nervous as he felt. Jesse was psyched that Savannah had decided to quit the soccer team to concentrate on football. She'd gotten better with every kick during the past week of practice.

Savannah tucked her hair behind her ears and slid on her helmet. Her kickoff was long and low. It skipped past the Glen Forest runner, forcing him to race back after the ball. When the Franklin defense tackled the runner at the 15-yard line, their bench exploded in cheers.

"All right, Savannah!"

"That's how to pin them back!"

"Hold 'em, defense!"

Jesse gave Quinn a shoulder bump and Savannah a high five. "Great kickoff! Our opponents aren't starting at midfield for a change."

Franklin and Glen Forest settled into a back-and-forth struggle. The Panthers scored first. They were at the 20-yard line when Jesse faded back to pass. Finding no one open, he scrambled, still hoping to pass. But he saw some daylight and took off. With Langston giving him a key block downfield, Jesse scooted past the Glen Forest secondary and was gone.

Touchdown!

As Jesse celebrated with his teammates, he thought about the next play. He wondered if Coach would let Savannah try for the extra point.

A Franklin player sprinted onto the field

with the answer. "Coach wants you to run I-35."

The Glen Forest Eagles stopped that running play cold. But the Franklin Panthers were still ahead, 6–0.

Glen Forest came back after another good kick and drove downfield for a score, but they didn't make the 2-point conversion after the touchdown. The score was knotted up, 6–6.

Shortly before halftime, Jesse dashed to his right and tried to throw a long pass on the run to Langston. The ball stayed in the air too long and floated short. The Glen Forest safety grabbed the ball for an interception at midfield. Glen Forest took advantage of the turnover to score again and grab the lead, 12–6.

Coach Vittone caught up with Jesse as the teams walked off the field at halftime. "Remember, Tark, it's tough to throw a long pass when you're running sideways. Get your feet under you first."

Jesse nodded. "I guess I thought I could

throw the ball like Jay."

Coach Vittone put his arm around Jesse. "Don't worry about being like your brother. Play your own game...your way. You're doing fine. We can come back in the second half."

They did. Jesse and his teammates on offense started moving the ball, picking up first downs but no scores. Then with only a few minutes left in the game, Jesse led the Panthers on a long drive, mixing runs by Griffin between the tackles and quick, short passes.

The drive stalled on the 15-yard line. Third down, ten yards to go.

Jesse stepped into the huddle. "Deep out on one." Jesse knew it was a tough pass. But he also knew his team needed a big play. "Give me enough time," he said to the Franklin linemen.

"Ready...set...hut one!"

Jesse faded back, avoided a Glen Forest tackler, and shifted right. He planted his feet and let fly. The ball wobbled a bit and seemed to take forever getting there, but it found Langston in the corner of the end zone.

Touchdown! The game was tied, 12–12.

His teammates were jumping up and down, but Jesse was looking to the bench. The Panthers had a chance to pull ahead if they could make the extra point. Coach Butler held his hands over his head and shouted, "Time! Time out!"

The offense huddled near the sidelines. "Let's have Savannah kick it," Quinn suggested. Jesse shot a surprised look at his best friend. It seemed Savannah had convinced even Quinn that she could kick.

Coach Butler shook his head firmly. "She hasn't practiced that much yet. I don't want to put the whole game on her shoulders." He grabbed his clipboard. "Let's run I-35 again. On one, let's go."

Jesse didn't move. "Coach, they stopped that play for no gain last time. Let me fake it to Griffin on the I-35 and roll out."

"What?"

Jesse grabbed the pen and scribbled some extra moves on the clipboard.

FAKE 35, BOOTLEG RIGHT

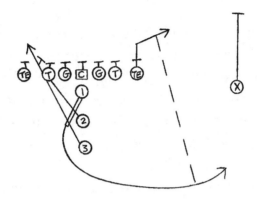

"Quinn and I have done this a dozen times practicing at the park," he pleaded with the coach. "Quinn'll be at tight end. He'll hold his block for a count of one and do a short down-and-out."

Coach Butler traded a look with Coach Vittone. They both seemed skeptical.

But then Butler said, "Okay, if you guys have been practicing it, let's give it a try."

The boys sprinted back onto the field. "Hey, Quinn," Coach Vittone called after them. "Don't forget to tell the referee you're lining up at tight end!"

"Ready...set...hut one...hut two!"

Jesse turned, faked the handoff to Griffin, and rolled right. When he looked back, a Glen Forest linebacker was rushing right at him. Jesse spied Quinn running free in the end zone. He floated a pass over the defender's head and into Quinn's waiting hands. Jesse was smiling even as the Glen Forest linebacker smashed him to the ground.

The Panthers were ahead, 14–12!

Savannah boomed the kickoff almost to the end zone, pinning Glen Forest deep in their own territory. The Eagles didn't have a chance to go the more than 80 yards against the fired-up Panthers defense in order to score. Time ran out and the Franklin High freshman football team had their first win!

As the team walked off the field, they all seemed happy: Langston about his big touchdown catch. Quinn about his game-winning extra points. Savannah about being the Panthers' new and improved kicker. And last but not least, Jesse, who was still remembering his big plays—a touchdown run, a touchdown pass, and the game-winning play.

He took off his helmet and shook out his sweaty hair. "Some of us may not look like we can play the parts," he said to the happy Franklin Panthers, "but I think we're putting together a pretty good football team."

Chapter 12

The trees along the highway were ablaze in October colors: reds and golds against the stubborn deep greens of the pines.

"What time is the game?" Jesse asked.

"One o'clock," his father said, turning to face him from the passenger's seat.

"Do you think Jay will get to play much?"

"Some. The coach has been using him as a fifth defensive back on passing downs."

"He said he was playing special teams too," Jesse's mom added, keeping her eyes on the twisting road.

Jesse slid down in the backseat. Part of him still saw his brother Jay as the quarterback, the main guy on the team. It was going to take some time to get used to seeing him as a safety and a part-time player.

As the Wagners pulled closer to the campus, the autumn woods gave way to the sights and sounds of a small college town. Stone and brick buildings, some more than a hundred years old, stood back from the tree-lined streets. Clusters of students and parents walked across the wide campus greens toward the football stadium.

Jesse's mother parked the car and they all stepped out. "It's a perfect day for a football game," she declared, looking up at the fluttering leaves.

"Yeah," Jesse agreed. "This game is going to be totally cool."

"Even though Jay isn't the quarterback?" his dad asked.

"Well, it won't be perfect, but that's okay. He's playing college football," Jesse said, thinking about his own unspoken dreams. "Not many guys get to do that."

Jesse's mom hooked her arm into Jesse's and pulled him closer. "And we still have a quarterback in the family."

They walked through the postcard-perfect campus to the stadium. His dad handed three tickets to a man standing at the stadium gate. Jesse pushed his way through the turnstile. Inside, under the stands, an older man wearing a bright green windbreaker shouted, "Program, program, get your program!"

"How much?" Jesse's father asked.

"Five bucks."

Jesse's dad paid for the program and handed it to him. "Here you go. Look up your brother."

Jesse leafed through the program until he came to the team rosters.

ROSTER

8	Joseph Martinez	PK	5-10	170	Fr.
9	James Jackson	RB	5-9	195	Jr.
10	Webster O'Brien	QB	6-0	175	So.
11	Chet Morton	WR	6-0	180	Jr.
12	Jay Wagner	DB	6-2	190	Fr.
13	Kirby Park	P	6-0	185	Sr.
14	Jerome Cook	QB	6-2	215	Sr.
15	Clayton Whitmore	WR	6-4	205	Sr.
16	Zach Friedman	QB	6-1	200	Jr.

"Here he is. Number 12," Jesse said. "At least he still has a quarterback's number."

The stands were slowly filling as the Wagners walked up the stone steps and found their seats in a midfield section filled with fans wearing green sweaters, hats, and sweatshirts. Across the sun-splashed field, the fans were mostly in red. The two teams ran out onto the field and the fans on both sides stood and cheered.

"Go, Dartmouth! Go, Big Green!"

"Go, Big Red! Go, Cornell!"

Jesse's mother pulled at his father's coat sleeve. "There he is!" she shouted. Jesse could hear the excitement in her voice. "Number 12. Go, Green!"

Dartmouth jumped out to an early 14–0 lead on a couple of quick touchdowns, including the 65-yard return of a short, low punt.

"That's what happens when you don't have any hang time on your kicks," Jesse said to his father as the Dartmouth section celebrated. "The other team gets a big return."

Cornell scored just before the end of the half to pull closer, 14–7.

Munching hot dogs in the stands at half-time, the family went over the highlights of the first half.

"Jay got to play quite a bit," Jesse's mother said.

"That's because Dartmouth was ahead and Cornell was trying to catch up by throwing passes," his dad said.

Jesse wiped some mustard off his cheek. "Jay looks like he knows what he's doing at safety. I mean, he doesn't look like he's in over his head or anything."

"So far, so good." Jesse's dad finished off his hot dog and settled back for the second half.

As the teams ran out, his mom stood, bouncing and clapping. "Go, Big Green!"

Cornell came charging back right away. They tied it up with a long run and then pulled ahead with a 32-yard field goal, pushing the score to 17–14.

Then Dartmouth rallied. The Big Green drove down the field, eating up yardage and time on the clock. Dartmouth capped the drive when their quarterback zigzagged his way to the end zone on a 15-yard scamper. Dartmouth had the lead again, 21–17.

After the kickoff, Jesse's father studied the scoreboard at the end of Memorial Field. "Less than three minutes to go and Cornell's got to cover 70 yards for a TD." He was on his feet. "Hold 'em! Dee-fense! Dee-fense!"

Jesse looked down at the field. "Jay's going in!"

Cornell kept fighting. Two first downs put the ball in Dartmouth territory at the 45-yard line. The cheers from the Big Green fans grew more desperate.

"Dee-fense!"

"Dee-fense!"

"DEEEE-fense!"

On fourth down with only twenty seconds to go, the Cornell quarterback faded back and lofted a long Hail Mary pass into the end zone. For just a second the Cornell receiver looked open. Jesse watched as his brother rushed over, leaped high into the air, and swatted the ball away. The moment the football hit the turf, Jesse and his parents jumped up and cheered, joining the other overjoyed Dartmouth fans. Thanks to Jay, the Big Green had hung on to win.

After the game, the fans and players from both teams milled around the field as the sun slipped down behind the White Mountains. The last rays of sunshine bathed the stadium in an orange, reddish glow.

"Here he comes!" Jesse's mother shouted over the noise of the crowd.

Jay emerged, dirty and sweaty but smiling with the Big Green victory. Their mom rushed over and gave him a kiss, avoiding the eye black on his cheek.

"Great play at the end," their dad said, giving Jay a playful punch on the shoulder pad.

Jay laughed. "Oh man, I was so scared. If I had let that guy catch the ball, I don't think Coach would've ever let me play safety again."

Jesse watched his brother as he talked.

With his helmet under his arm and the number 12 on his chest, Jay still looked every inch a quarterback.

Chapter 13

Jesse's cleats clattered against the hard floor when he stepped out the Franklin High School locker room door. He studied the freshman team schedule on the Big Board. The scores of the team's games had been neatly filled in.

FRANKLIN HIGH SCHOOL FRESHMAN TEAM
[all games on Thursdays]

Date	Team	Time	Score
9/19	South Shore	3:30 p.m.	L 26-0
9/26	@ Pinewood	3:30 p.m.	L 21-14
10/3	Glen Forest	3:30 p.m.	W 14-12
10/10	Roosevelt	3:30 p.m.	W 22-12
10/17	@ Auburn	3:30 p.m.	L 30-14
10/24	@ Morgan	3:30 p.m.	W 21-16
10/31	@ St. Andrews	3:00 p.m.	W 28-6
11/7	Eastport	3:00 p.m.	

The Panthers had added three more wins after the Glen Forest comeback. Jesse had played well at quarterback. He had surprised everyone except maybe Coach Vittone with his scrambling, play-calling, and knack for finding open receivers while still on the run.

Quinn stepped up behind Jesse. "Four wins, three losses," he mused. "That's better than I thought we'd be at this point. One more win and we'll have a winning season. And you"—he nudged his shoulder against Jesse's back—"turned out to be a pretty good quarterback."

"You've been a pretty good tight end," Jesse said, poking Quinn in the ribs with his elbow.

"What about me?" Langston protested. "I've scored four touchdowns. That's as many as Griffin." He posed and flexed his right bicep. "Not bad for a little guy."

"And you're forgetting about me?" Savannah had just emerged from the girls' locker room in full practice gear. "Where would you guys be without your kicker?"

The four friends jogged out to the practice field. Jesse stopped short when he saw something he hadn't seen in weeks—Henry Robinson warming up along the sidelines.

"What's Henry doing here?" he asked. "I thought he was out for the season with his ankle."

"I saw him running down at Hobbs Park last weekend," Savannah said. "He looked okay."

"What do you think Coach will do?" Langston asked. "Are you going to lose your job?"

"I don't know."

Quinn hooked his thumb back toward the gym. "No way. Coach has seen the Big Board. We've been winning and scoring points big-time with Jesse at quarterback."

Jesse wasn't so sure. "Coach may not want Henry to lose his starting position just because he got hurt. I mean...that wouldn't be fair."

"Hey, Jesse!" Coach Butler called, waving his clipboard over his head. "Hustle over here."

"Looks like I'm about to find out," Jesse said.

"Tell him to keep you at quarterback," Langston called. "I'm getting to like playing wide receiver."

Jesse joined the coaches. Henry didn't look over at him.

Coach Butler got right down to business. "We're going to split the practice reps between you two at quarterback today," he explained. "I want to see how Henry's coming along. I'll play the guy who looks like he'll give us the best chance to beat Eastport."

The two quarterbacks nodded in silence. Jesse stood up as straight as he could. He felt small next to Henry. The same way he felt when he stood next to his brother.

"Okay, let's go," Coach Butler said. "Henry, you take the first reps."

Jesse started to turn away, but then realized he wasn't sure where he was supposed to go. Was he a quarterback? A wide receiver? Or something else?

"Hey, Tark!" Coach Vittone called.

The older coach came over and rested his hands on Jesse's shoulder pads. "Listen, you've done a great job all season at quarterback," he said, looking Jesse in the eye. "Coach Butler just wants to give Henry a chance...you know, after his injury. Do you understand?"

"Sure, I get it. But I mean...am I still, you know, a quarterback?"

"Of course you're still a quarterback, Jesse." Coach Vittone smiled. "Just keep doing what you've been doing—scrambling, passing, calling the plays, leading the team." He leaned in and lowered his voice. "My guess is that you'll be the starting quarterback against Eastport."

Jesse stood on the sidelines with his helmet off and watched as Henry ran through some plays with the Panthers' starting offense. Jesse hated to admit it to himself, but he secretly hoped Henry wouldn't do well.

Sure enough, Henry was rusty after more than a month on the sidelines. Most of his passes were either too high or too low.

Jesse just watched, trying not to smile.

"Okay, Jesse. Switch up with Henry," Coach Butler ordered.

Jesse stepped in, feeling at home under center after six games. The offense ran some crisp running plays. Then Jesse faked a handoff, faded back, and hit Langston on a square-in pattern. On another fake, Jesse rolled out and slipped a quick pass to Quinn right in the numbers. Finally Jesse dropped back and lofted a long pass to Langston sprinting in full stride on a deep post pattern.

"Great pass, Tark!" Coach Vittone shouted, making an encouraging fist.

After the day's practice, Coach Butler called Jesse and Henry over. The coach pulled up the hood of his Franklin High sweatshirt to guard against the late autumn chill. It was nearly dark and Jesse could hardly see his coach's face, but he could hear his voice.

"Good practice," Coach Butler started. He paused, looking for the right words.

Jesse knew exactly what *he* wanted him to say.

"I think we'll stick with Jesse at quarterback," Coach declared. "But we'll keep working with you, Henry, giving you some reps," he added. "Right now I think Jesse gives us the best chance to beat Eastport."

Henry nodded. Jesse could see the disappointment on his face. Jesse knew he would have felt the same way if their coach had made the other choice.

Coach Butler clapped the two boys on their shoulder pads. "It's not the worst thing in the world to have two guys who can play quarterback."

Chapter 14

Jesse leaned over the study hall table. His pencil scratched busily across a sheet of paper, spilling out complicated patterns of Xs and Os and lines. Jesse was concentrating so hard, he didn't notice when Quinn and Langston sat down.

"What's up?" Quinn asked. "You doing math problems?"

Caught by surprise, Jesse covered the paper with his elbow. "No. I'm just...you know...making up some...aah...football plays."

"Let's see." Langston reached for the paper.

Jesse hesitated.

"Come on," Quinn said. "What's the big secret?"

Jesse slowly spun the paper around to show his friends.

FAKE LEFT, BOOTLEG RIGHT

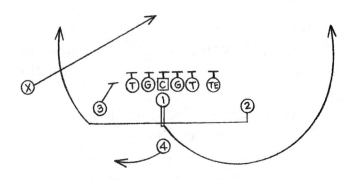

"I was just thinking," Jesse started to explain, "that Eastport's defense is supposed to be really—"

"Yeah," Quinn interrupted, "I heard they're awesome. They shut out Roosevelt, Glen Forest, and South Shore. They even stomped Auburn."

"Right, so I've been trying to draw up some plays to fake out their defensive players. I just came up with this. I figure we can fake it to Griffin going left," Jesse said, pointing to the diagram. "I'll keep it and run right. It's the old naked bootleg play."

Langston laughed. "You're gonna be naked?"

"Yeah, right." Jesse gave Langston a look. "No. It's just a play to get the Eastport defense going one way so we can run it the other way."

"What do you call it?" Langston asked.

"Fake Left, Bootleg Right."

"Cool." Quinn studied the play. "You know, maybe I could start blocking left from the tight-end position, then cut back and run a quick flare-out to the right." He grabbed the pencil out of Jesse's hand and scribbled a couple of lines. "You can hit me if I'm open. We can call it something like Fake Left, Bootleg Right, Tight-end Delay."

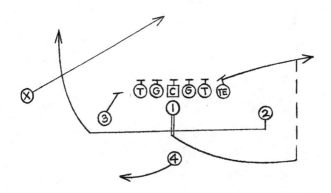

Langston looked at the papers spread out over the study hall table. "Have you got anything else?" he asked. "Like a play for *me*?"

Jesse picked up a piece of paper from a different pile and showed it to Langston.

Quinn leaned in for closer inspection. "What's this one?"

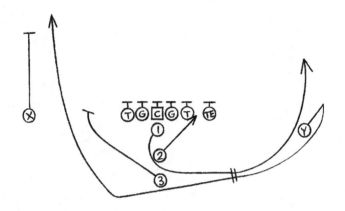

"It's a wide-receiver reverse." Jesse grabbed the pencil back from Quinn and used it as a pointer. "It's the same idea as the quarterback bootleg play. Get the Eastport defense chasing one way and hand it off to Langston going the other way."

Holding an imaginary football under his left arm and stretching out his right, Langston struck a Heisman Trophy pose. "And I run around left end for the touchdown."

"Are you going to show these plays to Coach Butler?" Quinn asked after the boys stopped laughing. "The Eastport game's coming up fast."

"I think I'll show two or three of the plays to Coach Vittone. See what he thinks first."

"Which ones?" Langston picked up some more plays.

"Probably the bootleg and the reverse."

Quinn held up the play he had drawn. "Don't forget to tell him about the tight-end delay pass," he insisted.

"Okay, okay." Jesse leaned back and held up his hands in surrender. "Why don't you guys make up your own plays?"

"Hey, *you're* the quarterback," Quinn said.

"Yeah, Coach Butler didn't think about putting Henry back at quarterback for long," Langston said.

Quinn nudged Jesse. "I think Vittone gave Butler the word. Coach Vittone loves his Tark."

Savannah slipped in beside the boys. "Hey, guys. You studying for Ms. Jackson's math test?"

Quinn held up some of Jesse's plays to

show Savannah. "Nope. Jesse here's not satisfied with just being the quarterback," he said in a teasing voice. "My man Jesse wants to be the head coach now. He's making up plays."

"Cool." Savannah's eyes skimmed over the plays—the quarterback bootleg, tight-end delay pass, and wide-receiver reverse. She tossed the papers back onto the table. "You've got plays for everybody but me."

"You're a kicker," Quinn said. "Kickers just kick. They don't really play football. Why would *you* need a play?"

Langston wasn't going to let Quinn dis Savannah. "Wait a second, she's a pretty good kicker. She's made..." Langston looked at Savannah for help. "How many points after touchdown have you kicked?"

"Nine in a row."

"Okay, okay, so she's a good kicker," Quinn said. "But who's ever heard of a play for a placekicker?"

The bell rang for the end of study hall. Quinn and Langston turned to leave.

"Wait, I think I've got one." Jesse quickly

drew eleven small circles in a placekicking formation. He added a row of eleven Xs all lined across the defensive front. Quinn, Langston, and Savannah hovered over him. Jesse added a few extra arrows and leaned back in satisfaction. His teammates smiled.

"Whoa, that's a very cool play."

"That's the best one yet."

"Super football fake-out."

Savannah put her hands in the air and shouted, "Touchdown!"

They all traded fist bumps.

Savannah looked at Jesse. "It's a great play, all right," she said. "But there's only one problem."

"What?"

"There's no way Coach Butler will ever let us use it in a real game."

Chapter 15

The football came spinning back. Jesse caught it, spotted the ball on the ten-yard line, and spun the laces away from the kicker. Savannah took two steps in and drove her right foot forward. Jesse heard the solid *plunk* of her foot hitting the ball. He looked up and watched it split the uprights.

"Good kick," Jesse said, pumping a fist.

Savannah smiled. "Eleven in a row."

Jesse checked the scoreboard as the Franklin offense jogged off the field.

DOLPHINS 04:00 PANTHERS
16 QTR 4 14

Franklin trailed the Eastport Dolphins 16–14 with only four minutes to go.

The Panthers had jumped off to a quick 7–0 lead in the first half. Jesse had scrambled right, set his feet, and launched a long pass. Langston had caught it behind the Eastport secondary and raced in for a 50-yard touchdown.

The Dolphins had come charging back. They'd ground out two long touchdown drives followed by a pair of 2-point conversions and grabbed a 16–7 lead.

"Eastport is undefeated for a reason," Quinn had said.

Now, after Griffin had scored the Panthers' second touchdown on a ten-yard run, Jesse wondered if the Panthers offense would get another chance to put some points on the board and win the game. "Come on, guys!" he yelled. "Hold 'em!"

Savannah nailed the kickoff, sending the Dolphins' kick returner scrambling back to the goal line. The Panthers pounced on the runner and pinned him down on the 18-yard line. The Franklin sideline was on its feet cheering.

"We need a three-and-out bad," Quinn said, pacing the sidelines like a nervous cat.

Jesse could feel the precious seconds ticking away and made some quick calculations. *Even if we force them to punt after three downs*, he thought, *we'll still only have two minutes—or less—to score.*

Jesse ran over to Coach Vittone. "How many timeouts do we have left?" he shouted.

"One. Coach wants to save it until *we* have the ball. We just have to hope we can stop them."

The Panthers defense came through. They stopped the Dolphins just one yard short of a first down, forcing them to punt. Jesse and his team would get one last chance.

The Franklin kick returner fielded the punt and weaved his way to midfield before being run out of bounds.

The Panthers' ball was on the 50-yard line with 1:40 to play.

Coach Vittone grabbed Jesse a few steps out onto the field. "Tark, start off with the naked bootleg play and then call the bootleg pass where the tight end cuts back."

Jesse raced onto the field.

"Call them both so we don't have to huddle after the first play!" Coach Vittone shouted after him.

Almost out of breath, Jesse called the two plays. He stepped to the line of scrimmage. The butterflies were back and swooping around in his stomach.

"Ready...set...hut one!" The Franklin line surged to the left. Jesse spun and held the football out for Griffin, the Panthers running back. At the last possible moment, he pulled the ball back and sprinted to the right.

The fake worked! Jesse had a clear field and took off. He was thinking *touchdown* when an Eastport defensive back leaped out and clipped his flying feet with a diving tackle. Jesse tumbled down at the 36-yard line.

First down!

But the clock was still running.

Jesse and the Franklin offense scrambled to line up for the second play. The clock was ticking: 1:02...1:01...

One minute left. The Panthers were ready to go.

"Ready...set...hut one!"

Again Jesse faked the ball to Griffin and spun to the right. This time, the Eastport defensive end wasn't fooled. He charged in on Jesse at top speed, but Jesse was ready. He lofted a pass over the defensive end's outstretched hands to Quinn, who was tackled right away at the 30-yard line.

The clock was still running! Thirty seconds...twenty-nine...twenty-eight...

Jesse looked over to the sidelines for the next play as the Panthers frantically tried to line up. Coach Butler was signaling him to spike the ball to stop the clock. Jesse waved his team into place as the seconds ticked away. "Come on, line up! Hurry up, hurry up!" Finally the Panthers were set.

"Ready...set...hut one!" Jesse slammed the ball straight into the ground to stop the clock.

The Panthers were down to their final chances.

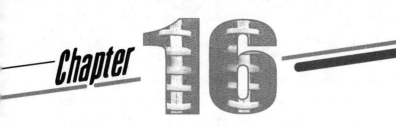

Chapter 16

Jesse could feel his heart pounding under his pads as he listened to Coach Butler and Coach Vittone.

He spotted Savannah warming up along the sidelines, kicking a football into a net. *That's right,* Jesse thought. *A field goal will win the game. We just have to get the ball close enough for Savannah to make the kick.*

Coach Butler summarized the situation. "Twenty seconds to go, third down, four yards to go for a first down."

"We still have one timeout," Coach Vittone reminded Jesse. "If anyone gets tackled inbounds, you have to call a timeout right away. We won't have time to line up and spike the ball again."

Coach Butler looked right at Jesse. "Let's go with Fake Post, Deep Out. Hopefully Langston can get some yardage and step out of bounds to stop the clock. If he does, we may still have time for two more plays."

Jesse swallowed hard. "Fake Post, Deep Out to Langston," he repeated.

"Be sure to step into it," Coach Vittone encouraged his quarterback. "Make a good, strong throw, Tark. You can do it!"

Jesse did exactly what Coach Vittone had said. Just as Langston broke for the right sideline, Jesse stepped into the throw and let fly a perfect spiral—almost as good as any pass Jay had ever thrown—on a straight line to his favorite receiver. Langston caught the ball at the 14-yard line and was tackled immediately. The side judge raced to the spot, windmilling his right arm.

Langston was inbounds! The clock was still running!

"Time out! Time out!" Jesse shouted, racing to the referee and frantically making the T sign.

Coach Butler and Coach Vittone were already on the field, studying the scoreboard.

"Seven seconds to go," Coach Butler declared. "We only have time for one more play."

"Maybe we can try a pass to Quinn in the end zone," Jesse suggested. "He's really tall. He can get his hands above everybody else."

Coach Butler shook his head. "They'll have a million guys back there defending against the pass. And if he's tackled short of the end zone, we don't have any timeouts." The coach was silent for a moment, deep in thought. "Savannah!" he shouted.

The Panthers placekicker rushed over. She already had her helmet on, ready to go.

"What's the distance?" Coach Butler asked Coach Vittone.

"The ball is on the 14-yard line, so we'll place down around the 22 for the kick. It'd be a 32-yard field goal."

Coach Butler turned to Savannah. "Have you ever—?"

"I've kicked a 35-yard field goal in practice," Savannah answered before the coach could finish his question. "A couple of times."

"Let's try it," Coach Butler said. "I think it's our best shot. Give her a good hold, Jesse."

Jesse and Savannah started back onto the field. "You know I only kicked those 35-yard field goals in practice," Savannah said in a nervous whisper. "I mean...no pads...no rush—"

"And no pressure," Jesse said, finishing her thought. Just short of the Panthers' huddle, an idea stopped him. He grabbed Savannah by the arm.

"Remember the play I made up for you the other day in study hall?"

"Sure."

"Let's run it."

"I...I...don't know..." Savannah was breathing hard. "No one else...knows the play."

"They don't have to," Jesse assured her. "In fact, the fake will work better if no one else knows about it."

Savannah stared at Jesse for a second,

thinking about the play, the kick, and the pressure. "Okay, let's do it."

The Panthers lined up for the field goal. Savannah took her steps back and nodded. Jesse knelt on the 22-yard line with his hands toward the center. He could see all eleven Eastport Dolphins on the line of scrimmage—just as he had drawn up the play in study hall—ready to rush in to block the kick. He almost smiled.

"Ready...set...hut one!

The ball spiraled back and Jesse caught it. But he only touched the tip of the ball on the ground for the briefest second. Instead of holding it in place for the kick, he flipped the ball over his shoulder without even looking.

Savannah didn't step forward toward the ball to kick the field goal. Instead, she dashed to the right, in back of Jesse, and caught his no-look, over-the-shoulder pass on a dead run.

The Eastport defense was completely faked out. All eleven players had rushed headlong to the spot where they thought

Jesse would place the ball, some diving in their efforts to block the kick. Now they could only watch helplessly as Savannah sprinted the 22 yards of wide-open field and into the end zone.

Touchdown! The Franklin Panthers had won, 20–16!

Jesse, Langston, Quinn, Griffin, Jenesis, Henry, Kurt, Denny, and all of the other shocked Panthers ran toward Savannah. They jumped up and down in a happy circle in the end zone.

"It worked! It worked!" Savannah yelled over and over as she held the football high above the celebrating mob of players.

Jesse threw his head back and laughed at the sky. "I can't believe it, Savannah!" he shouted. "Now you're a running back!"

Come on, Big Green, hold 'em!" Jesse yelled from the stands. He clapped his gloved hands together, more to keep them warm than to make any real noise.

"Do you want some more hot chocolate?" Jesse's mother asked.

"Sure, I'm freezing."

She passed Jesse a thermos cup. He blew on the hot chocolate and steam rose into the cold November air.

"Oh, that feels good," Jesse said after a couple of warm sips. "I think I'll pour some in my shoes. My feet feel like ice." He turned his attention back to the field. "We've got to find some way to stop that Princeton running back."

"Yeah," his father agreed. "He doesn't look very big, but he must have close to 200 yards today."

"I guess you don't have to look like a running back to run like one," Jesse said, thinking back to his own season at quarterback and Savannah's final touchdown run.

His father nodded and smiled. Jesse checked the scoreboard at the end of Memorial Field.

Dartmouth was leading 37–33 in an exciting, high-scoring game with less than three minutes to go. But the Princeton Tigers had the ball and were driving again.

"Look!" Jesse's mother pointed to the field and almost spilled her hot chocolate. "Jay's coming in."

"He's played a lot today." Even Jesse's father sounded excited.

Sensing that the next few plays would decide the outcome of the game, the Dartmouth crowd cheered loudly.

"Go, Big Green!"

"Hold that line!"

"Dee-fense! Dee-fense!"

The Tigers picked up two more first downs on quick passes to their star running back swinging out of the backfield. They were at the Dartmouth 24-yard line, but the clock was ticking away. There was just enough time for a few more plays.

"We've got to stop 'em," Jesse's father said, checking the clock nervously.

The Tiger quarterback faked a handoff to the running back. The Dartmouth defense surged forward, falling for the fake. The Princeton quarterback faded back and threw a deep out to a wide receiver who was open at the five-yard line.

Fearing the worst, the Dartmouth fans were on their feet. At the last second, the Dartmouth safety—number 12—dashed

115

over, leaped in front of the Princeton wide receiver, and snapped the ball out of the air. He tumbled to the ground, straining to keep his feet inbounds.

Tweeeeeet! The line judge rushed up, pulling both hands to his chest to signal a good catch.

"He got it!" Jesse's mother shouted, pounding her husband's shoulders and spilling hot chocolate everywhere. "He got it!"

"All right, Jay!" Jesse screamed into the late afternoon sky as his brother ran down the sidelines, holding the ball high in the air with one hand. With the crowd's cheers ringing in his ears, Jesse could almost see Jay beaming underneath the big green *D* on his helmet.

A minute later, the home crowd counted down the final seconds of the game.

"Five...four...three...two...one!"

Afterwards, the players stood around the field talking and shaking hands. The late autumn sun had already vanished behind the New Hampshire hills, leaving only the last rays of light lingering in the November chill. Jesse and his parents waited at the edge of the field.

"There he is!" Jesse shouted.

Jay walked toward them with his helmet pushed back, spinning a football in his hands.

"Is that the one you intercepted?" his dad asked.

"Yup, my first college interception."

"That was a fabulous play," his mom said.

"I knew he was going to throw the deep out," Jay said. He gave Jesse a sly wink. "Sometimes it helps to have played quarterback."

Jesse took off his winter coat and dropped it on the cold stadium turf. "Want me to go out for a pass?" He started out a few steps.

"No way," Jay said, flipping the ball underhand to Jesse. "I hear *you're* the quarterback now." Jay pulled his helmet down. "I'll go out for you." He ran a deep-out, dodging around the players and parents still on the field. Jesse stepped into the throw and spun a tight spiral right into his brother's hands.

"Touchdown!" their mom and dad yelled, throwing their hands into the air.

Jay walked back, grinning. "Not bad, little brother. Not bad at all," he said. "I think you're starting to look like a real quarterback."

For the first time ever, standing in the cold November gray, Jesse felt every bit as tall as his older brother. He finally felt like a real quarterback.

The Real Story

Coach Vittone knows his football. Fran Tarkenton was a fantastic quarterback. Listed at 6 feet and 190 pounds, but probably smaller, Tarkenton looked like a high school kid among the giants of professional football. But even though Tarkenton didn't look like a pro quarterback, he sure played like one.

In 1961, the Minnesota Vikings were a new expansion team in the National Football League (NFL). They drafted Tarkenton out of the University of Georgia in the third round of the NFL draft because they needed a quarterback. But they weren't sure Tarkenton could play the position in the NFL.

At that time, most NFL quarterbacks were "drop-back" passers. NFL quarterbacks took several steps back, planted their feet, looked for a receiver, and passed the ball before the defense could tackle them.

Tarkenton was different; he was a scrambler. Tarkenton moved around in the backfield, dodging tacklers and buying time so his receivers could get open. Then he would often toss them the ball while he was still on the move. Or sometimes he took off and ran with the ball. Tarkenton moved around so much that some called him "the Mad Scrambler."

Lots of so-called football experts thought Tarkenton wouldn't be successful with his scrambling style of play. They also thought he would get hurt running around so much. One day, they warned, a big defensive lineman would crush Tarkenton and his scrambling days would be over.

Boy, were they wrong. Tarkenton was terrific on the field. He completed 57 percent of his passes and threw for 47,003 yards and 342 touchdowns. Tarkenton also ran for 3,674 yards and 32 touchdowns.

Tarkenton was so elusive and quick on his feet, he almost never got injured. He played in 246 games over eighteen pro seasons. When he retired following the 1978 season, Tarkenton held NFL career records in pass attempts, completions, yardage, and touchdowns, as well as the records for rushing yards by a quarterback and wins by a starting quarterback.

Tarkenton's running and passing also turned his teams into winners. Even though the Vikings were an expansion team in 1961, four years later they had a winning record of 8–5–1 (eight wins, five losses, and one tie).

Following the 1966 season, the Vikings traded Tarkenton to the woeful New York Giants, who had won only one game that year. Over the next four seasons, Tarkenton and the Giants improved their record to 29 wins and 27 losses.

After the Giants traded Tarkenton back to Minnesota, the Mad Scrambler really took off. He led the Vikings to six straight winning seasons and three Super Bowls. Tarkenton was elected to the Pro Football Hall of Fame in 1986.

Fran Tarkenton wasn't the only undersized NFL quarterback. Drew Brees, who was also listed at six feet, led the New Orleans Saints to a 31–17 win over the Indianapolis Colts in Super Bowl XLIV (that's 44 in Roman numerals). In three seasons, Brees passed for more than 5,000 yards.

Russell Wilson isn't even six feet tall. He's listed at 5 feet 11 inches, but that hasn't stopped him from being a Super Bowl–winning quarterback for the Seattle Seahawks. Wilson uses his quick throwing action and football smarts to get the job done.

Athletes in other sports have done well despite not "looking the part." For example, Cal Ripken Jr. was a big man—6 feet 4 inches and more than 200 pounds. Most baseball people thought he was "too big" to play shortstop. Until Ripken, most shortstops were small, quick players who could scamper across the infield snagging ground balls.

Ripken started his major league career with the Baltimore Orioles as a third baseman. Then Ripken's manager, Earl Weaver, decided to go against the baseball experts' opinions and try Ripken at shortstop.

Like Tarkenton, Ripken proved the experts wrong. He was a terrific fielding shortstop. Ripken played thirteen straight seasons at shortstop, using his quick feet and long reach to snap up grounders and line drives. One reason Ripken could move quickly in spite of his size: he had been a top high school soccer player when he was growing up in Maryland.

While Ripken was considered too big to play shortstop, Tyrone "Muggsy" Bogues was thought to be too short to play basketball. Many professional basketball players are 6 feet 7 inches or even taller. Bogues was 5 feet 3 inches—more than a foot shorter than most of the other players. Bogues,

123

however, became an expert dribbler and passer. Because he was so short, taller players found it almost impossible to get the ball away from him. He was also very good at stealing the ball from his opponents.

Bogues played for more than thirteen seasons in the National Basketball Association (NBA). During that time, Bogues had almost five times as many assists (passing to a teammate who scores the basket) as turnovers (giving the ball to your opponent).

Just as some people think that only players of a certain size should play certain games, others believe that only males should play football. But according to the National Federation of State High School Associations, more than 1,800 girls in the United States played football for their high schools in 2012. The number has been growing for years.

Many, like Savannah, are kickers. And yes, it is true that one girl, Brianna Amat, kicked the game-winning field goal on the same night she was crowned Homecoming Queen at Pinckney High School in Michigan. They called Brianna the "Kicking Queen."

But girls are playing many different positions for their high school football teams. For example, in 2012 Erin DiMeglio became the first female to play quarterback in the history of Florida high school athletics.

You see, it's just like Coach Vittone said. In sports, it doesn't matter if you *look* the part. What matters is being able to *play* the part. So don't worry that you're too big or too small, or whether you're a girl or a boy. If you can help the team, you'll get your chance to play the part.

SPECIAL THANKS

The author wishes to thank
Steve Willertz,
a longtime youth football coach
from Severn, Maryland,
for his help with
the diagrams and
football terminology.

About the Author

FRED BOWEN was a Little Leaguer who loved to read. Now he is the author of many action-packed books of sports fiction. He has also written a weekly sports column for kids in the *Washington Post* since 2000.

For thirteen years, Fred coached kids' baseball and basketball teams. Some of his stories spring directly from his coaching experience and his sports-happy childhood in Marblehead, Massachusetts.

Fred holds a degree in history from the University of Pennsylvania and a law degree from George Washington University. He was a lawyer for many years before retiring to become a full-time children's author. Bowen has been a guest author at schools and conferences across the country, as well as the Smithsonian Institute in Washington, D.C., and The Baseball Hall of Fame.

Fred lives in Silver Spring, Maryland, with his wife Peggy Jackson. Their son is a college baseball coach and their daughter is a graduate student in Colorado studying to become a teacher.

For more information
check out the author's website at
www.fredbowen.com.

HEY, SPORTS FANS!

Don't miss these action-packed books by Fred Bowen...

Want more?

All-St★r Sports Story *Series*

.J.'s Secret Pitch
$5.95 / 978-1-56145-504-1

J.'s pitches just don't pack the power they need to strike out
e batters, but the story of 1940s baseball hero Rip Sewell
nd his legendary eephus pitch may help him find a solution.

he Golden Glove
$5.95 / 978-1-56145-505-8

Vithout his lucky glove, Jamie doesn't believe in his ability to
ad his baseball team to victory. How will he learn that faith
oneself is the most important equipment for any game?

he Kid Coach
$5.95 / 978-1-56145-506-5

cott and his teammates can't find an adult to coach their
am, so they must find a leader among themselves.

layoff Dreams
$5.95 / 978-1-56145-507-2

rendan is one of the best players in the league, but no
atter how hard he tries, he can't make his team win.

Vinners Take All
$5.95 / 978-1-56145-512-6

yle makes a poor decision to cheat in a big game.
omeone discovers the truth and threatens to reveal it.
Vhat can Kyle do now?

All-Star Sports Story
Series

All-Star Sports Story Series

Full Court Fever
PB: $5.95 / 978-1-56145-508-9

The Falcons have the skill but not the height to win their games. Will the full-court zone press be the solution to their problem?

Off the Rim
PB: $5.95 / 978-1-56145-509-6

Hoping to be more than a benchwarmer, Chris learns that defense is just as important as offense.

The Final Cut
PB: $5.95 / 978-1-56145-510-2

Four friends realize that they may not all make the team and that the tryouts are a test—not only of their athletic skills, but also of their friendship.

On the Line
PB: $5.95 / 978-1-56145-511-9

Marcus is the highest scorer and the best rebounder, but he's not so great at free throws—until the school custodian helps him overcome his fear of failure.

Check out **www.SportsStorySeries.com** for more info.